For my mother, Beatrice—B. B.

Copyright © 1990 Nord-Süd Verlag, Mönchaltorf, Switzerland
First published in Switzerland under the title *Valentino Frosch und das himbeerrote Cabrio*
English translation copyright © 1990 by Rada Matija AG

First published in the United States, Great Britain, Canada,
Australia and New Zealand in 1990 by North-South Books,
an imprint of Rada Matija AG, 8625 Gossau ZH, Switzerland.

Library of Congress Catalog Card Number: 89-43247
Library of Congress Cataloging in Publication Data is available.

British Library Cataloguing in Publication Data
Bos, Burny, *1944–*
Prince Valentino.
I. Title   II. Beer, Hans de, *1957–* III. Valentino
frosch und das himbeerrote cabrio.
English
823'.914 [J]
ISBN 1-55858-089-1

1   3   5   7   9   10   8   6   4   2
Printed in Germany

PRINCE VALENTINO

By Burny Bos

Illustrated by Hans de Beer

North-South Books
New York

Valentino the frog lived at the edge of a small ditch. He had no little brothers or sisters, so his parents spoiled him. His dad bought him lots of toys and his mother always called him "my little prince."

The trouble was that Valentino believed his mother. Whenever he saw his friends he would lean against his sports car and say in a high croaky voice, "I'm not a frog, like the rest of you—I just look like one. I'm really a *prince*! In a castle high in the mountains a beautiful princess is waiting for me."

Valentino's friends just laughed and made faces at him.

One night during dinner Valentino said, "Mother, isn't it funny that I'm a prince and you and dad are just ordinary frogs?"

His mother just shook her head and laughed. "You are a frog, Valentino. I just call you my 'little prince' because I love you so much."

"But in the castle high in the mountains the princess is waiting for me," muttered Valentino.

His father got angry. "Stop this nonsense!" he said in a loud voice. "You're not a prince and there's no princess in the mountains. Now eat or go to your room!"

After dinner Valentino hopped to his room. He sat down in a chair by the window and stared at the mountains.

Valentino became very lonely. None of his friends wanted to play with him anymore. They're just jealous because I'm a prince, he thought to himself.

But then one day while Valentino was swimming someone smeared mud all over his beautiful car. As he stared at the damage, a tear trickled down his face.

Then he jumped up and washed his car until it looked as good as new. He went home to get some food and set off to find the princess in the castle high in the mountains.

Valentino had just started his journey when he had to slam on the brakes to avoid hitting a little bird.

"Watch where you're going!" he yelled. "You should be careful when you cross the road."

The bird was so scared that she started to cry.

"Oh, stop crying!" said Valentino. "What's wrong?"

"I'm all alone," sobbed the bird. "I've lost my family and I don't know what to do."

"Well, I can't help you," said Valentino. "I'm on my way to meet a princess in the mountains and I don't have time for lost little birds."

But just as he was about to pedal away Valentino remembered that he was a prince. A prince must help his loyal subjects, he thought to himself. I can't leave this poor creature all alone.

So Valentino offered to let the bird ride with him.

"What's your name?" asked Valentino.

"Lucy!" chirped the little bird.

"Hop in," said Valentino. "I'm Prince Valentino."

Valentino and Lucy journeyed together for several days, but the mountains didn't seem any closer. Valentino didn't mind, because he liked being with Lucy.

They would pedal down the road under a bright blue sky singing songs and telling jokes until it was time to eat. Then they would have a snack and drink lemonade until it was time to curl up next to each other and go to sleep.

Lucy was growing very quickly. After just one week she was bigger than Valentino.

One night, before they went to sleep, Valentino told Lucy about the dangers of life. "We have many enemies," said Valentino. "Enemies who want to eat us." He told Lucy about snakes, hedgehogs, rats, and—worst of all—storks.

That night Valentino woke up suddenly. He heard something moving in the bushes. "Wake up!" he whispered to Lucy. "We have to hide!"

The two of them ran off and hid behind a tree. In the moonlight they watched a hedgehog creep out of the bushes and sniff Valentino's little car.

Each day they got closer and closer to the mountains and each day Lucy got bigger and bigger.

One day Valentino looked at Lucy's long sharp beak and became terrified that she might eat him. He quickly crawled behind the car to hide.

Lucy craned her neck and peered at Valentino. "What's wrong?" she asked. "Should I hide too?"

"Go away!" yelled Valentino.

Lucy was confused. They had been so happy together. Why was Valentino being so mean? "What did I do wrong?" she sobbed, as tears trickled down her cheeks. "I thought you liked me."

When Valentino heard Lucy cry he realized that he had made a terrible mistake. He crawled from behind the car and apologized to his friend.

But that night, when she went to sleep, Valentino tied a ribbon around her beak—just in case.

The next day Valentino and Lucy went swimming in the cool water of a big lake.

Suddenly, a stork landed in the water next to them. They quickly hid among the reeds until the stork flew away. Valentino was trembling. "That was close," he said. "Storks are *the* most dangerous creatures in the world."

Just as Valentino said this, Lucy looked down at the water. As she stared at her reflection, the little ribbon around her beak slipped off. "Valentino!" she shouted, "I'm a stork too!"

Valentino shook his head. "No you're not," he said. "You're my best friend. You just look like a stork. After all, I look like a frog, but I'm really a *prince!*"

Then Valentino plucked the ribbon out of the water. "We don't need this anymore," he said, as he threw the ribbon into the reeds.

At last, the two friends arrived at the castle. "This isn't quite what I expected," said Valentino. "There's no one here to greet me."

Lucy and Valentino looked at each other sadly.

"Well," sighed Valentino. "I guess I'd better go inside and meet the princess."

"I'll be all right," said Lucy. "I'm big enough to be on my own now."

Valentino looked up at his good friend. "I'll miss you," he said quietly. Lucy gracefully bent down and kissed him on the cheek.

"Hop on my back," she said. "I'll fly you over the castle wall."

In the middle of the courtyard on the other side was a large pool of water. "Goodbye Lucy," shouted Valentino as he leaped into the pool.

Valentino was shocked when he came out of the water. There was a long line of hundreds of frogs stretched around the courtyard.

"What are you doing here, little one?" said one of the frogs.

"I'm a prince," said Valentino. "I've come to meet the princess."

Everyone around him laughed. "Get in line, buddy," said a frog, gesturing over his shoulder with his thumb. "You're number 342!"

Valentino suddenly felt very small and lonely. There are lots of princes in the world, he thought to himself. I guess I'm not really special—I'm just a little frog.

One of the older frogs could see that Valentino was unhappy. "You don't belong here," said the frog. "Come on, I'll show you a secret passage out of the castle." The frog hopped into the pool and swam down to a tiny tunnel.

Soon, Valentino found himself sitting behind the wheel of his little car, pedalling as fast as he could toward home.

As he was winding his way down through the valley, Valentino heard a rattle and a bang and he knew at once that the chain on his pedals was broken.

He got out of the car and sat down by the side of the road.

Suddenly, he saw a bird swoop down out of the sky. It was Lucy!

"I see Prince Valentino needs some help," said Lucy with a grin.

Valentino looked down at the ground. "I'm not really a prince," he said softly. "I'm just a little frog."

"I know," said Lucy. "And I really am a stork. Can we still be friends?"

"Yes!" croaked Valentino happily. "You're my *best* friend."

Soon, they were ready to go home. Valentino tied one end of a rope around Lucy and the other around the bumper. Lucy flapped her wings and pulled the car down the road.

When they were very close to the little ditch where Valentino lived, Lucy stopped. "I think I should leave you here," she said kindly. "I wouldn't want to scare your parents."

As they said goodbye for the second time, Valentino took off his white scarf and tied it around Lucy's neck. He stretched up and kissed her gently on the cheek.

Valentino sat and watched Lucy as she slowly flew away and he didn't get up until she was gone. Then he hopped the rest of the way home.

Valentino's parents were overjoyed to see him. His mother hugged him and all his friends came over to ask about his journey.

"What happened?" asked his father.

"Well," said Valentino, "I found the castle and I learned that I'm not a real prince." Then Valentino smiled and said softly, "But I did meet a beautiful princess."